The Story of

Puss in Boots

Illustrated by Suzy-Jane Tanner

It's fun to Read Along

Here's what you do-

These pictures are some of the characters and things the story tells about. Let the child to whom you are reading SEE and SAY them.

Then, as you read the story text and come to a picture instead of a word, pause and point to the picture for your listener to SEE and SAY.

You'll be amazed at how quickly children catch on and enjoy participating in the story telling.

ISBN 0-86163-792-5

Copyright © 1987 Award Publications Limited
This edition first published 1995
3rd impression 1999

Published by Award Publications Limited,
27 Longford Street, London NW1 3DZ

Printed in Belgium

Puss

Boots

King

The Marquis of Carabas

Tom

Bag

Coach

Ogre

Farmer

The most beautiful princess in the world

There was once an old miller who had three sons. To the eldest he gave his 🌬️, and to the next, his 🐴. The youngest, Tom, was left with nothing but the 🐱!

"Do not worry," said 🐱. "Give me a pair of 👢, a 🪶 and a 👜. I will help you to make your fortune!"

was very surprised but he did as asked.

As soon as had pulled on his , he took his into the field and caught a young . Proudly hurried to the royal palace where he asked to speak to the . Upon seeing the king bowed low and handed the  to him.

"Here is a present from my master, the noble Marquis of Carabas," said .

The thought that must be very important to have such a fine servant. He could not have guessed that was the name had chosen for who was the miller's son.

"Please tell your master that I thank him," said the .

Every day took his and caught something to give to the as a present from . Whenever the asked about his master, clever would reply that was the richest and most handsome lord in all the land and that his was the finest that had ever been built.

The  longed to meet to see whether all that had told him was true.

Now, one morning  knew that the  would be driving by the river with his daughter, the most beautiful princess in the world. Just as he heard the  draw near,  told  to take off his ragged  and jump into the  .

"Help!" cried  . "My master has been robbed of all his  . I fear he will drown!"

When the  heard that was in trouble, he sent a servant back to his for a fine suit of . When had dressed, the invited him to ride in the royal .

 looked so handsome in his new clothes that the believed all had told him.

 fell in love with .

Meanwhile, ran ahead

of the  until he met some farmers working in the fields.

"Good ," said .

"When the passes, if you do not tell him that these belong to , you will be chopped into little pieces!" travelled on saying the same thing to everyone he met.

When the passed by, he heard, of course, that everything as far as the could see belonged to !

At last came to the of a rich and powerful ogre. "I have heard," told the , "that you can change yourself into any creature, no matter how big."

Suddenly, in the ogre's place, there stood a roaring . Frightened hid until the was himself again.

Now, all this time, had a plan to trick the . "It must be much harder," suggested , "to turn yourself into something as small as a ."

"You shall see," replied the and in his place, there scampered a tiny .

At once pounced on the and gobbled it up!

When the  arrived at the  gate  hurried to open it, "Welcome to the  of , Your Majesty," said .

The 👑 and 👸 were amazed to see such a fine 🏰 . But nobody was quite as surprised as 🎩 !

🐱 led them to where a splendid 🍽️ was waiting. This had been cooked for the 👹 but now, everything in the 🏰 and all the land for miles belonged to 🎩 .

The 👑 decided that 🎩

should marry if she
wished it, too.

The said that she did
so the arranged a grand
wedding for the very next day.
and were married
and they lived together happily
ever after.

became a great lord.
He had a different pair of
for every day of the

week, dined on the finest , and never chased a mouse again!